Terry Parks

Terry Parks

by Stanley
A.
Widney

Illustrations by Mary Stevens

Follett Publishing Company

New York   CHICAGO   *Toronto*

To my son Larry

Terry Parks

1

Salesman

Terry Parks had two sisters and no brothers. There was Angela, who was ten, and Kathy, who was six. Terry was in between, seven and a half.

The Parks moved into their new house in August. It was in the middle of a block of brand-new houses. There were lots of girls in the neighborhood, so Angela and Kathy liked it very much.

Terry liked the new house. He had a room of his own, and there was a vacant lot next door with a big sign on it that was very good for bounce ball and climbing.

But — there were no boys anywhere near his age for blocks and blocks, so it was pretty lonesome for Terry.

When he tried to get into the girls' games, they'd say, "Not this one. Go away, man child." or, "You can play in the next one. Beat it."

The only game they ever played with Terry was canasta, but after a while he began to beat them so often it wasn't much fun.

A half mile beyond the sign board there was a railroad track on which long freight trains ran. On each freight train, at the very end, there was always a little red caboose with a cupola on top.

All his life Terry had liked cabooses. He had three of them but they were just toys. What Terry wanted was a real caboose, right in his own back yard, so he could sit in the cupola and lean his head out of the window.

But whenever he mentioned it to Dad, Dad laughed and said, "Caboose?" in a way that made Terry know he'd just as well not say any more about it. All the same, Terry was sure, positive, that if he *did* have a *real* red caboose, with a cupola, he wouldn't be lonesome.

Dad Parks was a hardware salesman and had to travel a good deal away from home. When he was there, weekends, he played catch with Terry. Sometimes on Saturdays they would go to a ball game at League Park. Kathy went along once, but she ate so much popcorn and peanuts and hot dogs that she got sick and Mom wouldn't let her go again. That was all right with Terry. Kathy got her cheers and boos all mixed up. She booed the players and cheered the umpires.

On week days Terry played all by himself, bouncing his ball off the sign board or watching for the caboose on the faraway freight train. Or he played in his room, which was full of all kinds of building blocks, the plastic inter-locking kind — red ones for brick and white ones for stone or cement blocks, with doors and windows that locked in, too, and plastic picket

fence and garage doors that would open and close.

He loved to work with the blocks and became very good at it. Then one Saturday when the ball game was rained out, Dad built a long bench for Terry's room. It reached from one wall clear to the other, and on it they put a green carpet that looked exactly like grass. Terry called it his subdivision and pretended he was a contractor building lots of houses.

After he had eight houses all built, with a

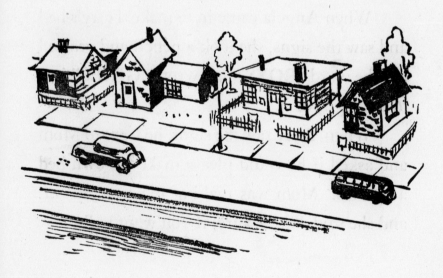

paved street and sidewalks of tile left over from
the bathroom, he made eight little cardboard
signs and glued them on the picket fences in
front of each house.

The signs looked like this:

When Angela came in to make Terry's bed
and saw the signs, she took a pencil and crossed
out the word "BOYS" and wrote "GIRLS" just
to the right of it.

When Terry saw the signs, he went to Mom
and asked if he could please make his own bed
after this. Mom was making the grocery list,
and she said, "Sure, sure, if you want to."

"Shall I tell Angela you said so?" Terry asked.

"Yes, yes, of course," said Mom, looking at an ad in the paper. "Just look at the price of hamburger. It's outrageous!" Then she looked up at Terry. "Oh, Terry? Did you want something?"

He just said, "Thanks, Mom. I'm sorry I bothered you at the groceries," and ran out to tell Angela.

Angela was so glad to get out of making his bed she invited him to join in a game of "Gloria, the Comet Girl." She was playing with Kathy and the Jones girls from across the street. Terry noticed they had made a Space Cruiser out of boxes, two barrels the dishes had been packed in, and four pieces of sewer pipe the men had left over when the street was put in. Angela had a large goldfish bowl for a

space helmet, and the other girls were using
pyrex mixing bowls held on with scotch tape.
It looked like a swell game.

Terry said, "Okay, I'll play. Am I the Cap-
tain?"

"Oh, no!" said Angela, "I'm Gloria the

Comet Girl. The others are my crew. You can be a man from Mars. We'll land there and capture you. We'll tie you up and take you back to Earth and make lots of money exhibiting you as a freak." Then she laughed, and so did the other girls.

Terry said, "No, thank you!" not very politely and went back to his room. He made eight more signs to paste over the others, and this time he added, *"Absolutely no Girls Allowed."*

Monday afternoon when Mom came in to vacuum his room, she took one look at his bed and said: "Oh! Just wait till I see Angela. She was supposed to make this bed and put clean sheets on it before school this morning."

"Oh, Jeepers, Mom," said Terry. "I didn't know about the clean sheets. I did make the bed though."

Mom looked at the bedspread with soiled sheets sticking from under it, dragging on the floor. "Why, it looks as if it had big python snakes under it — and a football and basketball too."

Terry went over and punched the wrinkles

and lumps under the spread. "Oh, they aren't snakes, Mom, but I may have put my basketball in there." He punched some more. "No, that's my pajamas," he said.

When he told Mom she had given him permission to make his own bed, she said, "What was I doing when you asked me?"

"Making the groceries list," he told her. He wondered why grownups always seemed to forget important things like that.

"That accounts for it." Mom nodded. She looked at his subdivision, "Well! You're good!"

Terry felt himself blush, and he felt very proud.

Mom bent down to read his signs. When she straightened up, she looked at him for a moment; then she put her arms around him and hugged him tight. "It's pretty tough being the only man in the family all week long, isn't it?"

She hugged him some more. Just before she left the room, she promised to make his bed herself after this.

The last Monday in August, while Terry was building his houses all over again with bigger yards that would have room for a toy red caboose in one of them and baseball diamonds and basketball courts in the others, he heard a motor running somewhere nearby. It buzzed and whirred and grunted and snorted.

When he got outdoors, Terry saw the biggest basement digger in the world, a million times bigger than the one Grandma had given him for Christmas, but with the same kind of bucket and crane and cab.

Angela and Kathy came out to see too.

"Oh, that awful noise!" said Angela.

"Oh, oh, what an awful noise!" said Kathy.

"Let's go down to Judy Brown's house so

we can't hear it," said Angela, and away they went.

Mom came to the window and said, "Oh, dear! I knew they'd build a house on that lot some day. Oh! Noise and dust!"

Terry found a box and sat on it. He watched the machine take great bites of the brown earth and dump it in trucks. When the trucks were full, they hauled the dirt away and came back for more. Terry watched them all afternoon till the men drove the basement digger up on a large flat trailer and hauled it away. The cab on the basement digger looked like a caboose on the trailer as it went down the street.

That night Terry had a dream. He dreamt the house next door was finished. Then came the best part of the dream. He saw a big moving van back up to the new house. The movers began to unload it. First, there were six bicycles; then a barrel full of bats, gloves, mitts, and a mask and chest protector. They brought out three double-decker bunk beds and on the foot-board of each bed was a name: "Bobby," "Jerry," "Dick," "Marty," "George," "Billy."

Next trip the movers brought six pairs of skis, six sleds, a basketball bangboard and six pairs of skates that looked exactly the same size as Terry's own.

When he woke up and remembered his dream, Terry got out of his bed and knelt beside it. "Let it be that way," he whispered. "Please let it be just that way, like the dream."

He got back in bed and lay there smiling for a while in the darkness, thinking how nice it would be with six boys living right next door. He was about to go to sleep when he happened to think of something. He hopped out of bed again and knelt down. He said, "Maybe you'd better make it five boys, or even three, so we can have the same number on a side."

Terry remembered every bit of his dream as he watched the first part of it coming true. By the middle of October the painters had finished and it stood there, just as it had in the dream, waiting for the moving van to back up and unload.

But the van didn't come. Every day after school Terry would run home to see. And when he was at home, every time a truck would rumble up or down the street he would run outside with his heart in his mouth. When the trucks went right on by, he'd feel like the whole world was sitting on his shoulders.

Then on Saturday, after ten whole days had passed, Dad looked up from the morning paper and said: "I see they're listing the new house for sale."

"What does that mean?" asked Terry.

"That they want to sell it," Dad said. "The house was built for a man named Roberts who has to move to another city now and can't keep it."

"Thank goodness," said Mom.

"That's what I say!" said Angela.

"Me, too!" said Kathy.

"What's everybody so happy about?" Dad asked.

"That's what I say," said Terry.

"Because," Angela told them, "Judy Brown knows the Roberts, and she told Mom and Kathy and me that there are *six boys* in that family!"

"Think of it," said Kathy, "two sets of twins eight and ten years old and two other boys, twelve and fourteen."

"The noise would have been deafening," Mom added.

Terry got up from the table and started for his room. They could hardly hear his "Excuse me."

"Terry!" Mom called after him, "Wait! You hardly sipped your orange juice and never touched your cereal."

"Back in a minute," he muttered, and ran on upstairs as fast as he could. He went to the bed and flopped down on his stomach. He tried very hard not to cry for a full fifteen minutes. Just when he was sure he'd have to, Dad came in with orange juice and cereal on a tray.

"How's about taking me to the stadium this afternoon, Pal?" Dad asked, putting the tray on the front lawn of one of Terry's houses. "State is playing the Aggies, and we can get seats right on the fifty-yard line."

Terry swallowed hard three times, then got up and drank all his orange juice without stopping. He looked up at his Dad and made an O out of his thumb and forefinger. "Oke, Pal," he said.

While Terry finished his cereal, Dad examined the neat row of block houses. "Nice work here, Terry," he said. "Which one is our house?"

"The one with the caboose in back," said Terry.

Dad looked at the toy caboose back of the house for a long time and kind of chewed his lip. He didn't laugh, either. Then he started talking about football, and pretty soon they went downstairs and Dad telephoned his boss, Mr. Dwight, about the stadium tickets. It was a keen game.

Sunday afternoon Terry watched the real estate men showing people through the new house. He was sure he had never seen so many little girls in his whole life. Every family that drove up seemed to have at least two girls. But not one boy did he see.

After the real estate men left, Terry went to the kitchen and found some wrapping paper. He took it to his room and cut a strip from it about six inches wide and two feet long. Very carefully he printed some words on it, saying, almost out loud, "I'll help them sell that house." On the way to school Monday morning he stopped by the For Sale sign at the new house and added to it a bit.

The first thing Terry noticed at school was two new boys. They looked like swell guys to him. He knew he was right when one of them said, "Hi. Do you play touch football at this school?"

"Hi," said Terry. "Sure."

"That's keen," said the new boy.

Just then Terry's teacher came up and asked the other new boy his name.

"Jimmy Thompson. I'm eight," he said.

"Where do you live?" asked the teacher.

"I don't know," he said, turning to the other new boy. "What shall I tell her, Dick?"

Dick said, "I'm his brother, Dick Thompson. I'm nine. We just moved here from Chicago, and we're living with our Grandma two blocks away at 6515 Lake Street till we can find a house. Dad has tried and tried to find a place near Grandma's, but we can't seem to find one for sale that suits us."

Just then the bell rang. Terry could hardly wait for recess. He cornered Dick and Jimmy at once, and he was so excited the words fairly jumped out of his mouth as he told them about the new house next door to his.

Dick and Jimmy were excited too. As soon

as the lunch bell rang, all three of them ran for Terry's house, and Terry got a box so the Thompson boys could look in all the ground floor windows.

"Just what we want!" they cried, and ran for their Grandma's house to tell their mom about it. Terry ate his lunch much too fast that noon.

The Thompson boys told him their mom

was very interested and that she and their father were coming to look at the house as soon as their father got through work at five.

After school Terry walked up and down the front porch waiting for them. It seemed as if five o'clock would never come.

But it did. The Thompsons and the real estate salesman got there within minutes of each other, and the salesman said, "Thanks, Terry." He showed them through the house, and they all stopped in the living room while the Thompsons signed some papers.

"That," said the real estate man to Terry, "was the quickest sale on record, and I have you to thank for it. After I talk with your father, you can expect a present to be delivered, with your name on it!"

Terry said, "Jeepers!" He was so happy he was numb.

Angela and Kathy had arrived in time to hear what the real estate man said. Angela grinned at Terry. "Lucky!" she said.

"I'll say!" said Kathy.

Mr. Thompson was walking around the front yard. He stopped by the sign board. He took off his hat and scratched his head, and then he said to the salesman, "Just a minute, here. I'm afraid if what this sign says is true, we're not wanted here."

"Oh, no!" cried Terry.

Everyone flocked around the sign and looked at it. Across the bottom of it was a strip of wrapping paper with words on it that read:

FAMILYS WITH BOYS WELCOME

"You see," said Mr. Thompson, "we also have two girls, Emily and Betty Jo. They're six and eleven. If they're not welcome here —"

The salesman looked at Terry. "What's the big idea?" he said, frowning. "Did you put that there?"

"I only wanted to help sell it," Terry said, his voice trembling. "I thought folks would see so many girls on this block they might think — well —"

Everyone was laughing now, except Terry, and he was feeling just awful.

Mrs. Thompson was telling Angela and Kathy that Emily and Betty Jo were staying with an aunt in Chicago so they could finish the first half of school there. Dick and Jimmy had both had measles in September and hadn't started school anyway, so they had come along.

Terry tried to explain to Dick and Jimmy.

"Huh!" said Dick, scornfully. "Girls!"

"They won't bother us," said Jimmy. "Let's play."

"Boy!" said Terry. "Say, I know a swell game. It's called Gloria the Comet — I mean, Jerry the Comet *BOY!* We've got a space ship all rigged up back there with helmets and everything —"

2

The
Pigeon Hole Desk

Terry and the Thompson boys were trying to build a caboose out of boards left over from their houses. It was the second Saturday in November, and a north wind was blowing so hard that the caboose would tumble over every time they got it set up.

Before long their fingers were freezing.

"It wouldn't be a *real* caboose, anyway," said Terry.

"My Dad says," said Dick, "if a fellow works hard enough at it, he'll aways get what he wants most. Why don't you work harder at getting a real caboose?"

"With a cupola," said Jimmy. "For Christmas."

"Everybody laughs," said Terry.

"We don't," said Dick. "Come on, let's go down in our basement. They brought Dad's desk in that noon load. We'll play office."

The Thompson basement was cluttered with packing cases and one small desk. The boys used the packing cases for walls. Terry stood and stared at the desk.

Dick and Jimmy seemed to be having a wonderful time playing office.

Terry was, too. Just being with the boys made him happy all over, but the desk fascinated him.

"Stop looking at the desk and come over here," said Dick. "You're supposed to be a salesman from out of town trying to get in to see the boss. What are you selling?"

"Hardware," said Terry, but he stayed by the desk. "Say," he said, "did you guys ever hear of a pigeon hole desk?"

"Pigeon hole desk?" said Dick. "No."

"There are lots of pigeons in Chicago," said Jimmy. "They're birds."

"Why?" asked Dick.

"My dad wants one. To check up on his sales when he comes home on Friday nights. He said he wants one with a roll top and pigeon holes."

"They coo," said Jimmy.

"Come on, let's play," said Dick.

"Your desk made me remember it," said Terry. "Monday is Dad's birthday. I just thought of something else. Dad's boss, Mr. Dwight, has a farm with pigeons."

"When they're little they're good in pies. They call 'em squads," said Jimmy.

"Squabs," corrected his brother. "Aw, come on, Terry."

Terry shook his head. "I have to go downtown, if Mom'll let me. Maybe I can get Dad a pigeon hole desk for his birthday."

The Thompson boys followed him to the door. "When you come back," said Dick, "I'll show you our train books. There's lots of cabooses in them. In color."

"Swell," said Terry.

Mr. Dwight was all alone in his office at the factory when Terry came in that afternoon.

"Well, Terry," he said with a big smile, "your mother called and said you were coming, but she didn't know what you wanted. What can I do for you?"

"Well, sir," said Terry, "Dad's birthday is Monday, and he needs a desk for the basement so we won't bother him when he's doing his homework — for you. And I guess he wants to raise a few pigeons."

Mr. Dwight had been nodding and smiling pleasantly as Terry talked, but when Terry said "pigeons," his eyes flew open like two window shades snapping up at the same time.

"Pigeons?" he said.

"Yes, sir." Terry nodded, "He wants to keep them in the desk, so he wants a desk with pigeon holes in it. I've heard him say so lots of times."

Mr. Dwight's face got so red that Terry

began to worry. The man's cheeks puffed out and his eyes almost went shut.

Then he began to laugh. He threw back his head and laughed up at the ceiling. He bent forward and slapped both knees and laughed some more. He took out his handkerchief, blew his nose, wiped his eyes, and chuckled and chuckled while he cleaned his glasses.

Terry's face felt very hot, and he wanted to swallow all the time. He stood on one foot and then the other. His eyes burned.

Finally Mr. Dwight looked at him again. He stopped chuckling quite suddenly and cleared his throat three times. He got up and took Terry's arm. "You come with me, Terry. I think we have just the desk you want."

All the way out to the store room, Mr. Dwight talked about what a fine man Dad was and how proud he should be of a boy like Terry.

He asked about Terry's school work and his
plastic building block hobby. By the time they
got to the desk, Terry felt fine again, and when
he looked at the desk he felt simply wonderful.

It was a light brown color, very large, and

when Mr. Dwight rolled the top up, Terry could
see two little doors on both sides. In the center
there were two slots, one above the other, to
slide sheets of paper in. There were two small
drawers next to the slots, and on each side of
the drawers were three holes, about five inches
high and two and a half inches wide.

Mr. Dwight pointed to the holes and cleared
his throat; then he said, very quietly, "Those
are pigeon holes, Terry. They're for cards and
envelopes and such. Why they're called pigeon
holes I don't know, but they are."

Terry felt pretty funny inside, like he'd
swallowed a baseball and it was stuck in his
throat. He swallowed hard and looked up at
Mr. Dwight.

"Dad loves to feed pigeons in the park,"
he began. "I — I don't know much about them,
except to look at. I guess maybe I should have

thought about it some more. You — you think
I'm pretty dumb, don't you?"

"I do not!" Mr. Dwight was emphatic. "I
was the dumb one for laughing like that.
Humph!" He blew his nose hard and stepped
back. He put his hands on his hips and looked
at the desk. "You think it'll go through your
doors, Terry?" He rubbed the end of his nose
with his pointer finger. "I think it will. Your
doors are good and wide."

Terry was about to say he was sure it would
when he suddenly remembered something.
"How — how much will you charge me for it,
Mr. Dwight?" he asked.

Mr. Dwight looked up at the cobwebby
rafters of the store room. "Well now, let's see,"
he said, rubbing his nose again. "How much
do you have to spend on it?"

Terry's voice was pretty small as he answered, "I've saved a dollar twenty from my allowance. Mr. Gruber gave me and Dick and Jimmy a quarter apiece to rake the leaves at his old house. That's a dollar forty five. I — I also have five dollars the real estate man gave me — but — well, I was going to get Mom a Christmas present —"

"Hold it!" said Mr. Dwight. "Sold! A dollar forty five is the figure I had in mind. We won't quibble."

Mom, Angela, and Kathy would hardly believe Terry had really bought the desk.

But Monday afternoon a big truck backed up to the Parks home just after school. There was a driver and another man. The driver said, "We had to take some chicken feed out to Mr. Dwight's farm first. It got the desk all dusty. Sorry."

They had to take the door at the head of

the stairs off to get the desk down in the basement. It was hard work, but they made it.

Just as they pushed it through the basement
door, Mr. Dwight drove up. He came down
and helped push the desk over in a corner.
"There, how's that, Terry?" he asked.

"Oh, swell!" Terry said. It did look mighty
fine — except for a lot of dust from the chicken
feed sacks that had been piled on it — and there
were little bits of cracked corn sticking in the
cracks of the roll top.

"That top doesn't lock too well," the truck
helper told Mr. Dwight. "I had to shut it
twice."

"That's okay," said Terry. "Dad can fix it."

Mom came down with a cloth and started
dusting the desk.

Suddenly she stopped.

"What was that?" she asked.

"What was what?" asked Mr. Dwight.

"I heard the funniest sound. Kind of a gurgling. There's something in that desk. Listen! There it is again!"

They all heard it this time. The truck driver grabbed the desk top and rolled it up.

Mom screamed.

There, in one of the pigeon holes, was a big fat blue pigeon, pecking at a piece of corn and cooing!

The truck driver said: "I remember a flock of pigeons lighting on the truck. They're always doing that because of the chicken feed."

But Terry and Mr. Dwight didn't hear him say it. They were laughing. They laughed so hard they grew weak.

"What's so funny about that pigeon?" Mom asked.

"Yeah, what?" asked Dick Thompson. He and Jimmy had just come in.

"What?" asked Jimmy.

Mr. Dwight stopped laughing long enough to say, "It's a secret between Terry and me. Isn't it, Terry?"

3

The Puzzle Expert

The Sunday after Thanksgiving Terry and the Thompson boys ran all the way home from church. In front of Terry's house they slid to a halt on the new-fallen snow.

"Right after dinner," Dick said. "We'll stack 'em up and wrap 'em nice, and Dad will take us over."

"I'll bet we have the most," said Jimmy.

"Who cares who has the most," said Dick, "just so our group wins. Come on, Jimmy. So long, Terry."

"See you right after dinner," said Terry.

Mom was in the kitchen putting on an apron so she could start dinner.

Terry said, "Mom, we've some jigsaw puzzles, haven't we? We didn't throw them away when we moved, did we? Thompsons didn't."

"In the attic, dear," she said, "but be sure to take off your good clothes. Attics get dusty even in new houses."

Terry changed as fast as he could. He put on a heavy sweater too, since it would be cold in the attic.

Just as he got to the attic door, Angela and Kathy came upstairs. It always took them longer to get home from church, because they had to stop and talk to so many girls.

"What are you going in there for?" Kathy asked.

"He's going to stick his head out of the window and play like it's the cupola on an old caboose," said Angela.

Terry ignored her. "This is very important," he said. "The boys in our group are collecting jigsaw puzzles to give to the war veterans in the hospital for Christmas." He opened the attic door. "Jimmy and Dick are getting theirs together, and their Dad will take us to the church basement after dinner. If we get the most, we each get a pair of genuine army surplus flier's goggles."

"Say," said Kathy, "Judy Brown said her Grandpa's a jigsaw puzzle fiend."

"That's right," agreed Angela. "And he left for Chicago to live just last week. Judy's

Mom said she had to get rid of a dozen boxes of them."

Terry shut the attic door. "I'll go get 'em right now," he said.

"No, I will," said Angela. "It's a good cause."

"I'll go with you," said Kathy.

"Never mind," said Angela, starting downstairs.

Kathy looked after her and made a face. "Oh, you're always too drippy to play with me when you're speaking to Judy. I wish the Thompson girls would hurry and get here."

Terry scratched his head. "Crazy girls," he said. "Only last week Angela and Judy had a big mad on."

"Oh, sure," Kathy said, "they get mad and make up every time the wind changes. I hope I'm not like that when I'm ten."

"You will be," said Terry. "Will you help me look for puzzles after you've changed?" Kathy was a good pal sometimes when Angela wasn't around.

By the time he found the paper carton in which the puzzles were packed, Kathy was beside him, dressed in blue jeans and one of Mom's old sweaters ten sizes too big for her. She rolled up the sleeves and said, "You take the puzzle boxes out, and I'll stack them up."

"We'll have to check them to make sure they're all there. The pieces, I mean," said Terry.

"Let's take them downstairs, then," said Kathy. She shivered, "I'm cold already."

They carried the puzzles, still in their boxes, down to Terry's room. He took his block houses down and put the pieces in a large tin can with a sign on it that said: "Potato Chips."

Then they put the six boxes of puzzles on the bench and looked at them.

"Good gravy!" exclaimed Terry. "These puzzles have over a thousand pieces in them. How'll we ever get them counted?"

"Why count?" asked Kathy, dumping the funny shaped pieces out of one box. "We'll work them. That's more fun." She started turning them right side up.

"Okay," said Terry. "Look. I've found a

couple of pieces that fit together already."

"Me, too," said Kathy. "Watch for edge pieces."

Terry stepped back and looked at the huge pile of pieces they hadn't even turned over yet. He said, "Listen, Kath, it'd be quicker just to count them." Then he spotted the picture on top of the puzzle box; the same as the puzzle would look, finished. It was a bright red caboose. "I *would* kind of like to work it, though," he said.

Time went fast as they worked and worked on the puzzle.

Dad Parks hadn't come home from church with the rest of the family. He had stayed for a business meeting. When he did come home, Mr. Dwight was with him.

Terry and Kathy heard them come in the hall downstairs.

Then they heard Dad call to Mom out in the kitchen,

"Oh, Mary! Mr. Dwight is with me."

"Oh. How — how very nice!" Terry didn't think Mom's voice sounded as if she thought it was nice at all. "Is he staying for dinner?" she asked.

"Oh, no," came Mr. Dwight's voice. "I just stopped by to pick up an important paper your husband was good enough to prepare for me last night."

Terry remembered Dad saying he had worked till midnight on an estimate for the boss. They heard Dad and Mr. Dwight come into the living room.

"What in the world is all this?" came Dad's voice. "What are you people doing?"

Kathy grabbed Terry's arm. "Let's go see," she said. They hurried downstairs to the hall.

In the living room they saw Angela sitting at the desk working a jigsaw puzzle.

In the dining room, Grandma was bent over another puzzle that must have had at least two thousand pieces.

In the kitchen they saw Mom working still another puzzle on the breakfast table.

The whole house smelled as if the roast beef might have burned a little.

Angela spoke without looking up from her puzzle: "Oh, Dad. How do you do, Mr. Dwight? Why, Terry is collecting jigsaw puzzles for war veterans. I got these at Judy Brown's house. Look. I have almost half of this one worked already."

Dad said, "You didn't happen to see a sheet with a lot of figures on it around that desk, did you?"

"No, I didn't," said Angela.

Dad looked all around the desk and in all the drawers while Angela went right on working the puzzle. Then he went to look in his pigeon hole desk in the basement. Then up to his bedroom. He came back down and went in the dining room. Grandma said she hadn't seen the paper. He went in the kitchen. Mom said she hadn't seen the paper. Grandma and Mom went right on working their puzzles too.

Dad took off his overcoat and hung it in the hall closet, then took off his suit coat and hung it on the back of the chair Terry was sitting on.

Terry thought Mr. Dwight looked pretty warm in his overcoat, so he said, "Won't you take off your overcoat and sit down too, Mr. Dwight?"

Mr. Dwight looked at his wrist watch, "No, thanks, Terry, my wife is waiting in the car." He looked at Dad, and Dad looked at him.

Dad said, "I'll find it in a minute, Sam."

He went upstairs again, saying, "I might have
left it in the bathroom."

When he came back down, Mr. Dwight
had his overcoat off and was helping Grandma
with her puzzle.

Dad stood in the hall between the living and dining rooms with his hands on his hips and said, "I dare say those puzzles are very interesting and important. Well, I have a puzzle of my own, and Mrs. Dwight is waiting out in the car. Will someone please help me find that paper?"

Mr. Dwight went to the front window and looked out, then came back and picked at Grandma's puzzle some more. "She's reading the Sunday paper," he said.

Mom, Grandma, and Angela all said, "I'll help you in just a minute," and kept right on puzzling.

Terry thought somebody had better help Dad, so he started to get out of his chair. As he did so, he felt something crisp and rattly brush his shoulder. It was a sheet of paper, folded lengthwise, in Dad's coat pocket.

Dad was saying, "I'll count to ten. If those puzzles aren't moved aside so I can look for that paper under the table covers and desk blotter by the time I get through, I'll move them myself. One. Two —"

Terry tugged at Dad's shirt sleeve, "Dad, I think I can solve *your* puzzle."

Dad stopped counting and turned to Terry, "You can?"

"Sure," said Terry, "isn't that it in your suit coat pocket?"

Dad looked so funny everybody started laughing. He had put the paper there to give it to Mr. Dwight at church and had forgotten all about it. Terry had never seen Dad's face so red.

Just then a car horn honked out in front.

Mr. Dwight grabbed his coat and the paper. He said, "Thanks for finding the paper,

Terry. Say, if you'll come over to my house this afternoon, I'll give you a dozen or more puzzles. I buy 'em all the time."

Terry turned around to ask Dad if he would drive him over to get them. Dad was helping Angela with her puzzle.

Sunday dinner was very late at the Parks home that Sunday, and it was served buffet style.

Terry was afraid the Thompsons might have gone on without him. When he finished eating he went out on the porch. Dick Thompson was standing on their porch.

"Ready?" asked Terry.

"Nope," said Dick. "We haven't even started dinner yet."

"Why not?" Terry could almost guess.

"Puzzles," said Dick. "All over the tables, puzzles."

4

Musician

Terry sat astride an empty packing barrel in Thompson's basement. Jimmy stood in front of the barrel and made the thing rock by pushing down and lifting up on it. Dick stood at the back and rolled the barrel from side to side.

All three of them were wearing cowboy

hats and twin holsters with six-shooters in them. Terry and Dick wore cowboy boots. Jimmy had a pair of his mother's high-heeled slippers with a pair of his Grandpa's old spats over them. He was expecting cowboy boots for Christmas.

Terry was supposed to be riding a bucking bronco at a rodeo. "Yip-ee!" he yelled, hitting the back of the barrel with his hat.

Dick stopped rolling the barrel and came around where he could see Terry's face. "Cowboys yell louder than that. What's the matter with you today?" he asked.

Jimmy stepped back, and one of his boot-slippers fell off. Disgustedly, he said, "Aw, he's got the birthday blues. Hadn't you heard, Dick?"

Dick had been to the barber shop getting his hair cut all that Saturday morning. "Did I miss something?" he asked.

"Terry snooped," said Jimmy, sitting on the floor.

"I did not," said Terry. "It was an accident. Mom and Dad didn't know I was upstairs, and I heard 'em. Mom said I could carry a tune better than Angela or Kathy."

"He means sing," said Jimmy.

"Then Dad said our old piano looked out

of place in a room full of modern furniture," Terry continued. "Mom asked if we couldn't trade it in on a new one and Dad said no because we couldn't afford any more payments on account of the new house. And then, oh, brother!"

"Go on," said Dick. "And then what?"

"Mom said she was going to have Madam Gartola give me music lessons for a birthday present!" Terry groaned.

"You mean that lady with the awful perfume that comes to school and smells up the music room?" asked Dick.

Jimmy nodded. "Her fingers make me think of hot dog buns when she plays piano at assembly."

"She broke a piano bench just sitting on it last Thursday," said Dick.

"When she counts 'one, two, three, four,'

it makes me think of a seal I saw in a zoo barking," said Jimmy.

"And she baby-talks you!" Dick rolled his eyes.

Terry shrugged his shoulders and hung his head. "What can I do about it? I have to do something."

Dick looked at Jimmy, and Jimmy looked at Dick. They nodded wisely. Dick said, "Now listen, Terry. You do as we say. You go upstairs, and when you go through the kitchen, you yell back to me and say, 'Sure, it will go through here all right.' My mom will ask you what, and you say, 'a piano.'"

"What for?" asked Terry.

"Oh. We didn't tell you that, did we? Because at breakfast Mom told Dad we ought to have a secondhand piano in the basement. It's going to be a game room, see? We left our old game room piano in Chicago because it pulled apart when they tried to move it out."

"And you think your folks might buy ours?" Terry asked.

"If it's worked right. You know how grown-ups are when you come right out and ask them something."

"Sure," said Jimmy. "That's why I've been wearing these slippers and spats. A while ago Mom told Dick she guessed they'd just have to get me some real boots. See?"

The Thompson boys gave Terry a few more instructions; then he went upstairs. Mrs. Thompson was in the kitchen. Terry pretended not to see her as he yelled back, "Sure, it would go through here."

"What would go through there?" asked Mrs. Thompson.

"Oh, hello, Mrs. Thompson. A piano.

The boys said you were thinking of getting one for down there," Terry said.

"Yes, we were," she said, wiping her hands on a dish towel, "but it would have to be second-hand. Do you know of one?"

Terry rubbed his chin and looked at the ceiling. "Well," he said slowly, "I've heard some talk at home about our piano not matching the furniture. I don't know —"

Dick and Jimmy came running upstairs. "Come on out front, Terry," said Dick. "Got something to show you."

Out on the porch, Dick said, "That was plenty. Now you go home and wait. Mom'll be there in ten minutes."

Jimmy made an awful face. "Madam Gartola! Boy! I can smell that perfume right now."

Terry's conscience began to hurt a little

bit on the way across the snow-covered lawn. Mom was awful good to him most of the time, and he hated to deceive her. Maybe he'd better talk to Dad about it.

When Dad heard the whole story, he thought awhile and then said, "I think maybe we can talk Mom out of those piano lessons if we go about it right. Now, look. You go in the house with me, talking about how much you'd like to play some other musical instrument, like a — a —"

"A drum! Trap drums!" Terry said. He could just see himself pounding away on a set of drums and cymbals.

"Drums?" Dad's eyebrows shot up, then he frowned. "No, no! Drums are out. You'd drive us crazy."

"Harmonica?" Terry ventured. He liked harmonica players on TV.

Dad thought Mom might not consider the harmonica a musical instrument.

They finally settled for a clarinet. Terry thought that would be fine. He could march with the school band and get in all the games free.

As soon as Mom heard them talking about Terry's wanting to play clarinet, she smiled all over and said, "Clarinet? Why Terry, I had no idea! That's a fine instrument. Uh — you run along and play with Dick and Jimmy. I want to talk to your father."

Terry lingered on the porch long enough to hear her say, "Now, if that isn't the strangest coincidence. Mrs. Thompson was just on the telephone. She said she wondered if we intended to keep our old piano in our nice living room with all the new furniture, or take it down in the basement. I wondered what she was driving at till she said they intended to get one and wondered if we'd ever measured the basement steps to see if it would go down."

There was a long pause; then Mom said, "I wonder if the Thompsons would give us enough for that old piano to buy a secondhand clarinet?"

That very evening Mr. Thompson brought two men out from the plant where he worked.

They had a platform on iron wheels that they called a dolly. With the help of Terry's Dad and Mr. Thompson, they pushed and carried the old piano around the sidewalks and, after removing four different doors, managed to get it into the Thompson's basement.

Monday, December seventh, was Terry's birthday. His eighth. First off, Kathy had to have *her* present. Her birthday was in April but when she was little she always had presents on every other person's birthday or she cried. Now she was too old to cry, but Dad and Mom got her something anyway, just for old times' sake.

It was a cocker spaniel puppy, two months old and pretty well trained. Her name was already "Lady." She was black and very hairy, and Dad said, "She's really for the whole family." But Kathy hugged Lady and said, "She's

mine! She's mine!"

Terry didn't mind. He saw the detective kit he wanted lying on the sideboard.

And he wasn't a bit surprised when Mom handed him a leather case first and said, "Here is your number one present, dear."

He put the clarinet together and tried to make a sound on it. He did. A horrible, squeaking sound that made everyone grab their ears.

Dad said, "Hey! Leave that thing alone till you learn how to play it!"

"Oh," said Mom. "I've already arranged for his lessons. Terry, dear, you'll be so glad to know that Madam Gartola will take you right after the first of the year. I'll bet you didn't know she was a clarinet teacher too, did you?"

5

Private Eye

The detective kit was lots of fun. It was so much fun that Terry didn't mind too much when the Thompson boys went along with their father to Chicago to bring their sisters home for Christmas.

In the kit was a magnifying glass; a pair

of shell-rimmed glasses with a big rubber nose fastened to them; a badge like a real detective's, only it was smaller and the printing on it read, "Junior G-Man"; a pretty good gun that clicked twice when the trigger was pulled; and a fingerprint outfit.

The fingerprint outfit was a dandy.

There were sheets of paper with spaces to write the name, sex, color of eyes, color of hair and the crime the person being fingerprinted was supposed to have committed.

Under that were five squares, one for each finger on one hand, and one for the thumb. The suspect's fingerprints were put there, after first having been pressed on the ink pad.

The ink pad was in a tin box. The instructions on the lid read, "The ink in this pad is harmless to skin or fabrics and will wash off easily in plain water."

When Terry asked Mom what that meant, she said, "Oh, why do they make such things for children to play with?" But she explained what it meant and tried the ink on her own fingers, and sure enough, it washed right off.

The Thompson boys didn't leave until school vacation started on Saturday the nineteenth of December, so Terry had plenty of time to fingerprint both of them. And he finger-

printed everyone in his own family, including
Grandma and Lady.

To fingerprint Lady, Terry used just four
of the squares on her page; one for each paw.
Then he showed them to her. Lady said
"Woof?" and made a few tracks on the hall
runner before the ink rubbed off.

About ten o'clock Monday morning, Terry
was playing "Private Eye" in his room. He
played that he was a railroad detective and was
riding in a caboose, in the cupola, watching for
a train robber to get on. Then somebody
screamed. It was several seconds before he re-
alized it was his mother instead of a robber who
had screamed.

He ran downstairs as fast as he could, and
his sisters came running from wherever they
had been.

"Oh, dear! Oh, dear!" Mom moaned. "It's

broken! Smashed to smithereens! Mother! You come in here too!"

Grandma was shaking throw rugs on the front porch. She poked her head in the door and said, "I'm out here enjoying this nice warm sunshine. Smells like March instead of December. Thawing like everything."

When her three children were around her in front of the fireplace, Mom said, "Look at my lovely flower bowl!" She was almost crying. "It's the one I made and painted with my own hands to give to Aunt Pansy for Christmas."

Mom went to adult classes in ceramics and spent many evenings at the high school building working with clay and paint. Her ash trays, vases, and bowls were all over the house and in all of her relatives' houses.

"Someone dropped it or knocked it off the

mantel. I want to know who did it!" Mom said.

Grandma spoke from the door. "Land sakes, all that fuss over a gob of patted mud."

Mom said, "If you only knew the hours I've spent . . . Angela!"

"I didn't do it, Mother," said Angela. "Why, I haven't dusted in here for a week."

Mom ran a finger over the mantel shelf and looked at it. "I can believe that all right. How about you, Kathy?" She spoke sternly. "Have you been bouncing your basketball in here, or playing with Lady?"

"Oh no, Mama," Kathy said. "Lady and I have been playing outdoors all morning."

Mom looked at the mud on Kathy's shoes and said, "I can believe that, too. Well, Terry?"

"I've been in my room all morning playing private eye. I haven't been near the fireplace. I've been working on my disguises."

Mom looked at the big nose and shell-rimmed glasses Terry was wearing and said, "There's no doubt about that." She had to laugh a little bit because Terry looked so funny. She shrugged. "Well, what's done is done, but I sure would like to know who broke that bowl."

After Kathy had gone back outdoors with her galoshes on and Angela had gone to the kitchen to finish drying the breakfast dishes before she started dusting and Mom had gone to telephone her best friend, Marion, who also made things out of clay, Terry went to work.

He gathered up the pieces of broken clay and examined them carefully through his magnifying glass. He found one good print in a dusty place on a large piece that had part of one handle still on it.

Then he climbed up on a kitchen chair and examined the top of the mantel. He found several good prints there that looked exactly like the one on the piece of bowl.

Next he walked to the center of the room, faced the fireplace, and stood very still while he carefully looked at every piece of furniture as he tried to work out just how the crime was committed.

He went to the davenport and found some-

thing on the cushion nearest the fireplace and said, "Ha!"

On top of the back of the davenport he found something that made him say "Ha" again.

From there he went to the top of Grandma's high-back plush chair just to the left of the fireplace. He examined that carefully and said, "Oho!" and snapped his fingers. "I've got it."

He ran upstairs for the fingerprint charts he'd made the day before, brought them down, and spread them out in a neat row on the coffee table in front of the davenport.

"Mom! Grandma! Angela!" he called, "I've solved the Case of the Broken Bowl! Come in here!" He went to the door and yelled, "Kathy! Lady! Come in here!"

He had to call all of them several more times before they finally came in. Mom said

good-by to Marion on the phone as soon as he
called her, but it was ten minutes before she
hung up.

Angela always read a comic while she wiped
dishes and couldn't come till she found out if
Gloria the Comet Girl got out of that cave on
Jupiter.

Kathy had to stop on the back porch and
take off her galoshes and wipe Lady's feet with
one of Terry's old worn-out T-shirts.

Grandma was the last one to join the
group in the living room. "What nonsense is
this?" she demanded.

Mom said: "Detective Sergeant Terry
Parks has called all the suspects together. He
claims to have the case solved, but his evidence
is not conclusive. He believes the guilty party
will confess, however."

Terry laughed and said: "Aw, Mom!"

Then he made his face very sober behind the rubber nose and big glasses.

Angela said, "Of all the silly twerps you are the twerpiest. Do I have to stay here, Mother?"

Mom just nodded.

Kathy said, "Did I have to wipe Lady's paws off just to come in here and look at that goofy face?"

Mom said, "Sit down, dear."

Lady sat down too and scratched behind one long ear with a hind paw. "Woof!" she said, disgustedly.

Terry cleared his throat, "Ahem! I shall now perduce the guilty party who busted —"

"Broke." Grandma corrected.

"— broke the cemeratic bowl."

"Ceramic, dear," Mom said gently.

"Yes," said Terry. "I call your attention

to exhibit **A**." He held up the dusty piece of
bowl with the handle on it, "I find a print here
that is very clear. A muddy print, too. Through
the magnifying glass the flecks of mud can be
seen — here and here." He lifted one on the
point of a pencil. It was quite a large fleck.
"See the mud?" Terry was looking down at
everyone's feet as he spoke.

Kathy said, "Terry Parks! If you think
that I —" She held up her hands. "See, Mom?
There's no mud on my hands, and I sure didn't
climb up there and kick that thing off with my
foot." She made a face at Terry.

He acted as if he hadn't even heard her.
He walked to the davenport and pointed to the
cushion. "See this tiny piece of mud here?"

Mom looked and said, "Why, that is mud!
Who —"

"Please, Mom, just a moment," said Terry.

He pointed to another bit of mud on top of the
back of the davenport, "Here is another, and
here —" he pointed to the top of the back of
Grandma's high-back plush chair — "here is
still another."

Everyone was saying "Oh" and "Ah" and
"Well, I didn't do it!"

Terry pointed to the mantel shelf. "Up there, in the dust, you will see several prints. Wait till I've finished, please. Do not disturb the evidence."

Grandma said, "I should have dusted up there myself."

"All right, Terry," said Angela, "make it snappy. Why would Kathy want to touch that vase or bowl or whatever it was?"

"Me?" Kathy glared at Angela. "Angela Parks! I bet it was you, and you —"

Mom said, "Now, girls!" She turned to Jerry, "I'm afraid this has gone far enough, Son. Just whom are you accusing of breaking that bowl?"

"Oh, no one!" he said. "I'm only trying to get the facts, Ma'am. Just the facts."

"I'll facts you in a minute," said Angela.

"Now," said Terry, "everybody think.

What was in that bowl last?"

Everyone thought, and they all remembered at once. They said, "Candy!"

Terry nodded. "Right! That's where Mom put the last batch of my birthday fudge. Candy!" he repeated.

He had to jump back then as a black streak shot past his legs, up on the davenport, to the

back of its top, and then to the top of the back of Grandma's high-back plush chair. It skidded to a stop on the far side of the mantel, right where the bowl had been.

Lady sat there waving her stump of a tail and barking as she had learned to do when anyone said the word "candy."

Terry raised a hand and turned it over. "There's your bowl breaker," he said.

Everyone laughed then and congratulated Terry, except Kathy. She was crying. "Mom, Mom! It was my fault. About an hour ago I told Lady I wished we had some candy. She ran in here and stayed a long time. I'm so sorry."

Mom put her arms around Kathy and said, "There, there, dear. It's everyone's fault for feeding Lady candy. I'll make another one in next week's class. Forget it — but you teach Lady not to climb things in this room!"

Terry felt pretty proud of himself. He went upstairs and put Lady's fingerprint chart on his desk. Under the puppy's prints he wrote:

"One convixion. Bole braking. Patroled to Kathy Parks on good bahaver."

6

The Grandfather's Clock

Jimmy and Dick got home the next day. Terry went over as soon as Mom would let him to tell them about solving the mystery of the broken bowl. They laughed, and Dick said, "Smart work, boy!" Then he introduced Terry to his sisters, Emily and Betty Jo.

Terry said "hello," and they said "hello," and then went over to the Parks house to meet Angela and Kathy. The boys thought that was a very good idea.

Then Dick said, "Did you ever get your Christmas list written?"

"Oh, sure," said Terry. "Long ago."

"So did we. Did you order a caboose, Terry?"

"We saw a caboose," said Jimmy.

"Nope," said Terry. "Even Santa Claus would laugh at that, I bet. Everyone does."

"We don't," said Dick.

"On the back of a freight train, it was," said Jimmy.

"I heard Mom tell Dad that cabooses are a fixation with me," said Terry.

"What's a fixation?" asked Dick.

"I don't know," Terry admitted. "It isn't

good though. I could tell by the way Mom
said it."

"It had a cupola on top," said Jimmy.

"What did your Dad say?" asked Dick.

" 'Hummmm.' He just said, 'Hummmm.' "

"Is that bad or good?"

"I don't know. Sometimes it's good, sometimes it's bad," Terry said.

"There were men in it," said Jimmy.

"In the cupola of the caboose?" asked
Terry.

"No," said Jimmy. "On the back platform.
I wish you *did* have a caboose in your back
yard. With a platform."

"Don't I!" said Terry, with a big sigh.

"The thing to do," said Dick, "is to get
your Mom something she wants awful bad and
give it to her the day before Christmas Eve."

"We did that last year," said Jimmy. "We

wanted skis, and she didn't think we should have 'em. She wanted a new food mixer. All four of us kids got her one from our savings. We got the skis."

"Ski boots too. Worked keen," said Dick.

"I know what Mom wants," said Terry, "but where'd I ever get her a grandfather's clock?"

"And wool ski socks, too. Boy! I wish it would snow again. Which one of your Grandpa's clocks does she want?" Jimmy asked.

"It's not any Grandpa's clock," said Terry. "It's a grand*father's* clock."

"That's what I said," said Jimmy.

Dick had to explain to his brother.

"You mean a big tall clock as tall as you are?" Jimmy asked.

"Taller," said Dick.

"That's it," said Terry.

"I know where there's one," said Jimmy. "Don't you remember, Terry?"

All three boys remembered then. "At Mr. Gruber's!" said Terry and Dick together.

"Sure," said Jimmy. "In his old haunted house."

"Aw-w-w," said Terry, "it isn't haunted. Remember? Mr. Gruber said it wasn't when he showed us the inside."

"When we raked his leaves," said Dick.

"We only went on the porch and looked up the stairs," said Jimmy. "You couldn't drag me in there."

Terry sighed. "Mr. Gruber wouldn't sell it anyhow."

"Let's go ask him," said Dick. "Come on. The sun's shining, and he always sits out in front of the house where he rooms when the sun shines, even in winter."

"I can't go," said Jimmy. "I have to go to the dentist." He opened his mouth and pointed into it. "Ga too wi caaee."

"He says he has a tooth with a cavity," said Dick. "Come on, Terry."

As they walked down the street toward the house where Mr. Gruber had roomed ever since his children grew up and moved away, Terry said, "I sure hope I can get that clock for Mom. Caboose or no caboose. She's wanted a grandfather's clock ever since I can remember."

When they got to the rooming house, sure enough, there was Mr. Gruber, all bundled up in a greatcoat and muffler, sitting in his armchair in the sun. Mr. Gruber loved boys and girls. He always had a cheery "hello" for them on their way to and from school, or any time. He seemed very happy to see Dick and Terry.

When Terry told him what he wanted, the

old man scratched his head and said, "Sell it? Well now, I'll tell you, I don't know if that clock's much good any more."

"Oh, that's all right," said Terry. "My Dad likes to fix things."

"Nope," said Mr. Gruber. "Wouldn't want to sell you something that wasn't working. Tell you what, though. I'll give you boys the key to my old house. Here it is, right here."

Mr. Gruber unbuttoned his greatcoat, then he unbuttoned his suit coat, then he unbuttoned his sweater coat. After that, all he had to do was pull up his pull-over sweater, and there, across his wide stomach on top of his vest, was a gold chain with a watch on one end, an Elk's tooth in the middle, and a bunch of keys on the other end. He took a key from the ring and gave it to Terry.

"There," he said, rolling down his pull-

over sweater. "Now you boys wait one hour."
He rolled up his pull-over sweater again and
looked at his watch. "It's eleven-thirty," he said.
"Eat your noon meal first and go to the old
house at exactly twelve-thirty. Got that?"

"Yes sir," said Terry and Dick. "Twelve-
thirty."

"Right. Unlock the door and go in. Shut
the door and go upstairs. Clock's right at the
head of the stairs. Open the door of the clock

and pull down on the right hand chain. Got that? Right! Then you give the pendulum a little push. Know what a pendulum is? Right! If the clock runs — you know, goes tick-tock, tick-tock — well-l-l — we might figure out a deal."

"Right!" said Terry. "Thank you, Mr. Gruber. Thanks!"

As the boys went down the street, Terry looked over his shoulder. Mr. Gruber was buttoning all his coats and things and laughing. Terry said, "Gee, that clock just has to work! It just *has* to."

As soon as he had eaten, Terry ran over to Thompson's. It was twenty minutes after twelve.

Dick met him at the door with a long face. "I can't go with you," he said.

"Aw, why not?" Terry was disappointed.

He wasn't exactly *afraid* to go in the old Gruber house alone. He was sure he didn't believe in ghosts, but — he wanted Dick along. "Why can't you go?" he asked.

"Music lesson," Dick said, holding his nose. "Madam Gartola!" He shook his head, and his voice was very sad. "She called Mom up and said she could take me on Saturdays, but would today be all right this week on account of Christmas? Mom said I would be delighted!"

Jimmy poked his head out the door. "Haw!" he said. He opened his mouth and pointed inside with his finger. "Ga hoo erry."

"He got through early," said Dick. "Lucky."

"I'll go with you as far as the porch, Terry," said Jimmy. "I wouldn't go inside even to get away from Madam Gartola."

When Terry and Jimmy arrived at Mr. Gruber's old house, it was twenty-five minutes after twelve according to Angela's watch. Angela had lent it to Terry if he would wipe the dishes that night.

Terry and Jimmy sat on the front porch for five minutes.

At exactly twelve-thirty, Terry put the key in the lock and gave it a turn.

"Squeeeek," went the old lock, but it turned.

Terry took hold of the door knob. It squeaked too. Then he pulled the door open. "Squeeeeeek!" went the hinges.

Jimmy shivered. "Boy!" he whispered, "is this ever spooky!"

Terry laughed. "It just needs oil. Stop being scared. We've been here before."

"Sure," said Jimmy. "I shivered then, too."

He pushed Terry from behind. "Go on in."

"I'm going," said Terry, "as soon as my eyes get used to the dark." He peered into the gloomy hall. "I don't want to fall over anything."

"Haw!" said Jimmy. "You're scared too."

"I am —" he stopped and swallowed. "I am not!" He squared his shoulders and stepped over the threshold. "Come on, Jimmy. The stairs are right here in front of us."

Jimmy jumped forward and grabbed the belt on Terry's storm coat. "Okay, go ahead. I can stand it if you can." But Terry noticed that his teeth were chattering.

"Let's go!" Terry started up, with one hand on the railing and Jimmy holding tight to his belt.

One step. Two steps. Three steps . . . and then . . .

Something groaned!

In two long hops, Jimmy was back on the front porch. Terry wanted to run too, but he had said he wasn't afraid. He made himself go another step. Again something groaned!

"Terry!" cried Jimmy. "Let's get out of here. You can buy her a pair of socks for Christmas."

But Terry was laughing! "Come on back, scaredy-cat," he said. "It's just these old stairs. See? I can make them groan any time." He put his foot on the fourth step, and sure enough, it was a loose board in the steps that made them groan.

"Haw!" said Jimmy. "I knew it all the time." He swaggered in. The boys ran all the way to the top together, and in a jiffy they were standing in front of the grandfather's clock.

"Say!" said Jimmy. "That's a pretty good

ol' clock. It's prettier up here than when we looked up and saw it that day. Look. As tall as I can reach up. Look at that carved wood on it. Looks like frost on the door, doesn't it?"

Terry felt very sad. He was afraid he couldn't buy it.

"Aw, don't give up," said Jimmy. "Dick said Mr. Gruber told you he might make a deal."

"Yes," said Terry. He began to feel excited again. "But we have to see if it works first." He took hold of the little bronze key in the door's latch — and then —

The clock spoke!

"Open me gently, my boy. I'm very old."

"What?" Jimmy yelled, grabbing Terry around the neck, almost choking him. "Who said that?"

"The — the clock!" Terry stammered. He

loosened Jimmy's hold on his neck. Terry was pretty frightened too.

"Do not be frightened, children," said the clock. "Go ahead and open my door. I will not harm you. But please handle me easy."

The boys were too frightened to move.

"I want to go home!" wailed Jimmy.

"Me, too," said Terry. "Clocks can't talk."

"This one **can**," said Jimmy. "Come on, Terry. Push me! My feet won't start!"

"Oh, I'm sorry I frightened you," came the voice. "I didn't mean to. Please. Do just as Mr. Gruber said and start me. Right?"

"R-r-right," said Terry. And then he thought of two things. There are no such things as ghosts — and — he had heard that voice before! His fear left him so fast he broke out laughing.

"Terry!" Jimmy cried. "Are you laughing or crying? We gotta get outa here!"

"Oh, relax, boy," Terry said, importantly. "The clock said it wouldn't hurt us. Didn't you, Mr. Clock? Right! Now let's just open the door like this —" He glanced over his shoulder at his chum. Jimmy's eyes were as round as a pair of half dollars, and his mouth was open.

Terry almost snickered as he reached for the right hand chain. "And we pull down on it like this — and we start the pendulum like this — there!"

"Tick-tock tick-tock!" went the old clock.

"Gee!" said Jimmy. His mouth was still wide and his eyes were popping. "It works! But I don't think your Mom would like it to talk."

"Oh, I don't think the talking goes with it," said Terry, looking all around the hall, "does it, Mr. Gruber?"

A closet door just to the right of the old clock swung open, and Mr. Gruber stepped out. He was laughing.

"Mr. Gruber!" Jimmy was jumping up and down and pointing. "It was you!"

"Yep." Mr. Gruber patted Jimmy's shoulder. "I'm sorry I frightened you. I just thought I'd have a little fun, that's all."

"Aw," said Jimmy, "I wasn't very scared—"

Mr. Gruber laughed and turned to Terry. "I'll have this clock brought over to your house. I had Mr. Emerald, the jeweler, come up and look at it a half hour ago. It's in fine shape. Now when did you want it delivered? Christmas Eve, right?"

"The day before that," said Jimmy, quickly.

Terry shook his head. "No." He said. "I can't do it that way." His heart was so full of gratitude to Mr. Gruber that he just had to tell the nice old man all about it. About the caboose and everything.

Mr. Gruber didn't laugh about the caboose. He just said "Hummmm," something like Dad. Then he said, "I reckon all of us have something we want real bad. Me, I always wanted a gold watch chain with an Elk's tooth on it when I was your age." He started unbuttoning all of his coats, then he rolled up his pull-over sweater and showed the chain and Elk's tooth to Jimmy, who hadn't seen it.

"Boy!" said Jimmy. "I'm glad my tooth the dentist worked on this morning wasn't that big."

Mr. Gruber laughed. "Right." Then to Terry, "You can see that I finally got what I wanted. But I had to learn a lesson first. That was to try to make others happy by doing things for them. I think you've about learned that lesson, Terry. I heard about your getting your dad that roll-top desk for his birthday."

"The pigeon hole desk," said Terry. "It only cost a dollar and forty five cents —" He stopped and swallowed. "But this clock —"

"It's already yours," said Mr. Gruber.

"I've been intending to give that clock to some good friend. I could never sell it, you know. It was my grandfather's grandfather's clock, and I want to know that it's being well cared for. I know your mom. Right? So the clock will be her Christmas present from you, and then all of us will be happy. Right?"

Terry thanked the nice old man a dozen times, and Jimmy did too.

"I'll always remember it's really your clock, Mr. Gruber," Terry said. "To myself I'll always call it 'Mr. Gruber's clock.'"

"Nope." Mr. Gruber put an arm around each of the boys and started for the stairs. "You don't need to say it that way, Terry Parks. You just call it, 'grandfather's clock.' Right?"

"Right, Grandfather," said Terry.

"Right," echoed Jimmy, as they walked down the creaky, groany stairs.

7

The Caboose

On the way home from Mr. Gruber's old house Terry and Jimmy were very quiet for a long time. Terry was so happy he couldn't talk. He was so glad for Mom that he had even forgotten his caboose until Jimmy mentioned it.

"I tried to tell you," said Jimmy, just as

they came to their block, "but you and Dick never pay any attention to me."

"Tried to tell us what?"

"About the caboose."

"What caboose? Oh, the one you saw coming from Chicago. Oh." Terry slowed down.

"That one. It was clear here that I saw it. Where the railroad yards are. Across from the plant where my Dad works. We stopped there. Dad and Dick went in the office, but I went over to look at the caboose."

"You did?" Terry felt excited. "Gee!"

"I asked the men where it was going," said Jimmy.

"Where?" asked Terry. "Where was it going?"

"To the junk yard. They said it wasn't much good any more and that was its last trip."

Terry stopped and grabbed Jimmy by the

arms. "Are you sure that's what they said?
You're not kidding me?"

"Sure not. They showed me the junk yard.
A lot of old freight cars and two cabooses,"
said Jimmy.

"Boy!" said Terry. "Oh, boy! Do you
suppose your Dad would let us ride out to the
plant with him in the morning? Would he?"

"We can ask," said Jimmy.

Terry didn't tell his parents he was going
with Mr. Thompson to see the cabooses in the
railroad junk yard Wednesday morning. He
just said he wanted to see the plant, which was
true. He did. But in his pocket was the five-
dollar bill the real estate man had given him.

Of course the boys asked Mr. Thompson if
they could explore the railroad junk yard. Mr.
Thompson asked the man in charge of the junk
yard if it would be safe, and he said sure, if the

boys would promise not to climb up the iron
rails on the sides of old box cars and would be
careful of splinters.

As soon as they were in the junk yard,
Jimmy stopped and pointed. "One of them is
gone. There's only one caboose now."

That was all right with Terry. One caboose

was enough for him. The boys climbed up the steps on one side of it and climbed down on the other. They climbed back up again and leaned on the black iron railing around the end and turned the iron brake wheel in the middle. They went inside the caboose and climbed up the wooden steps to the cupola and sat on the torn leather seats and looked out of the windows.

They climbed back down and looked at the place where a stove had been. They knew a stove had been there because the floor had coal spots and the wood on the wall back of it was cracked from the heat.

They wished the stove was there now, because it was growing very cold outside and a few flakes of snow were falling.

After about half an hour, Terry couldn't stand it any longer. He had to find out.

The boys went to the little house where the

boss of the junk yard sat on a chair by a little round stove. He was reading a paper and smoking a funny little pipe.

"How much for one of your cabooses?" asked Teddy.

The boss of the junk yard took off his funny steel-rimmed glasses and looked at Terry and the Thompson boys. "How's that?" he said.

Terry explained that he had five dollars to spend for a caboose.

The boss took out a big red handkerchief and blew his nose like Terry's new clarinet. After a while he said, "Ain't no good, the one that's left. Sold the only good 'un yesterday afternoon. Took it away on a flat trailer to fix it up, they said."

"Flat trailer?" asked Terry.

The boss pointed through a dirty window.

"Like that one," he said.

The boys looked through the window and saw a big semi-trailer like the one the men hauled the ditch digger away on when they finished digging Thompson's basement.

The boss said, "We give 'em away, the old cabooses. Yard'd be jam full if we didn't. Railroad's changin' to cabooses with bay windows, instead of cupolas."

"Aw-w," said Terry. He thought the railroads were making an awful mistake. Then he said, "You mean if I want one I can have it?"

"Sure," said the man. "If you can afford to have it hauled away." Then he added, "We keep the wheels, of course."

Terry and the others were out of the office quicker than you can say salamagander. They ran to the semi and looked for the driver. He was in a little café drinking coffee.

Terry showed him the five-dollar bill and asked him if he could haul the caboose to the Parks house for that.

The man started to laugh. Then he looked at Terry's face and didn't. "You want it pretty bad, don't you, kid?"

"I sure do," said Terry.

The man finished his coffee and stood up. "Christmas only comes once a year," he said. "What's a telephone number where I can talk to your father?"

Terry hadn't thought of that. His heart sank. "Oh," he said. "We'd better ask him, hadn't we?"

"Well," said the truck driver, "he might be a little surprised to find a caboose pulling into his driveway. What's the number?"

Terry told him, then held his breath while the man put a dime in the telephone and dialed the number. The man told Dad what Terry wanted, and then just stood there grinning and saying, "Yes. . . . I see. . . . I see . . ." He said "I see" a dozen times, Terry thought.

"What does he see?" asked Jimmy.

"Quiet," said Dick.

The man turned to Terry. "Your father wants to talk to you, Terry," he said.

Terry took the receiver and said "hello" in a very small voice.

Dad's voice said, "Now look, pal. It's beginning to snow. Let's just let this ride a few days, shall we? I'll promise you this much. You won't be sorry if you do."

Terry gulped. He could tell from his father's tone that there was no use to argue. He tried not to sound too disappointed as he said, "All right, Dad."

It was hard to be cheerful the rest of that day and the next, even if it was Christmas Eve. Lots of nice things happened to him, like the tree in the church basement when their group leader presented each of them with a pair of genuine army surplus flyer's goggles because they got the most jigsaw puzzles for the veterans, and the package from Grandma and Grandpa Parks that Mom let them open after they came home. Lots of nice things.

He had his arms full of presents when he went up to his room that night. But no caboose.

For the first time since he was four years old he cried himself to sleep, he was so heartsick — and he was ashamed of himself for being that way. He kept telling himself it was wrong — but it didn't do a bit of good.

In the morning when he woke up, about six-thirty, it was still dark outside. But not too dark, because it had snowed hard all night.

He heard Angela and Kathy get up and go downstairs to the fireplace where they had all hung their socks, near the Christmas tree. He heard them yell "Oh-h-h!" and "Ah-h-h!" time and again. He sat up in bed and looked through his window. He could see lights on at Thompsons all over the house.

He sighed deeply and then got up and put on his old bathrobe and his boots. He went in and brushed his teeth, and then went downstairs very slowly.

Everybody stopped talking and looked up at him.

They watched him go over to the fireplace and look at his lumpy sock. He knew that the lumps were nuts and Christmas candy.

But there was a white envelope in the top of the sock. Above it, on the mantel, there was a square box. He took the box down and

opened it. In it was a striped cap made of denim, like his jeans. There was a bright metal nameplate above the bill of the cap. Letters on it read like this:

FREIGHT

CONDUCTOR

Terry just stood looking at it. He felt numb all over.

Mom came over and took the cap. She put it on his head without saying a word, then took the envelope out of his sock and handed it to him.

He opened it slowly and drew out the sheet of paper it contained. He read:

"Dear Terry: Earlier this week I heard from the following friends of yours: A real estate salesman; a Mr. Gruber; a Mr. Dwight; a man who signed his name, 'The proud father of a very good and generous boy;' and

two boys whose names are Dick and Jimmy.
They told me what you wanted most. I could
not, due to its size, bring it down the chimney.
Please go take a look in the back yard."

And the letter was signed, "S. Claus."

Terry just stood there for a minute, staring
at the letter. Then he looked at Mom. There
were tears in her eyes. Dad had them too. So
did Angela and Kathy.

Terry ran for the back door. He bumped
furniture all through the house, but he didn't
even feel it. He flung open the back door and
looked.

And there it was, red, with steps and rails
on both ends — and a cupola on top. Instead of
wheels, it rested on big blocks of wood, but that
was all right. And it was lighted inside. The
row of windows glowed with light.

Up by the cupola there was a little black

chimney, and there was smoke coming from it.

Terry shut his eyes tight and looked **again.**
He hurried upstairs to get dressed.

Then he ran down the freshly scooped
path and climbed up on the platform.

Suddenly the back door of the Thompson

house opened, and Dick and Jimmy rushed out. They were wearing caps just like Terry's.

"All aboar-r-d!" yelled Terry.

Jimmy and Dick raced down the path and jumped up beside Terry on the platform of his very own red caboose!

DATE DUE